THE
READING CHALLENGE
FROM THE
BLACK LAGOON®

Get more monster-sized laughs from

The Black Lagoon®

THE
READING CHALLENGE
FROM THE
BLACK LAGOON®

by Mike Thaler
Illustrated by Jared Lee

SCHOLASTIC INC.

ABDO
Spotlight

"To readers everywhere" —M.T.

To those who taught me the gift of reading. —J.L.

BOOKWORM

ABDOPUBLISHING.COM

Reinforced library bound edition published in 2017 by Spotlight, a division of ABDO, PO Box 398166, Minneapolis, Minnesota 55439. Spotlight produces high-quality reinforced library bound editions for schools and libraries.
REPRINTED BY PERMISSION OF SCHOLASTIC INC.

Printed in the United States of America, North Mankato, Minnesota.
092016
012017

♻ **THIS BOOK CONTAINS RECYCLED MATERIALS**

ISBN 978-0-545-78521-1

Text copyright © 2015 by Mike Thaler
Illustrations copyright © 2015 by Jared D. Lee Studio, Inc.

LIBRARY OF CONGRESS CATALOGING-IN-PUBLICATION DATA

This book was previously cataloged with the following information:

Thaler, Mike, 1936-
  The reading challenge from the Black Lagoon / by Mike Thaler ; illustrated by Jared Lee.
  p. cm. -- (Black Lagoon adventures; #30)
  Summary: Hubie's class is having a reading challenge. Two teams will compete and whoever reads more books gets a special lunch with a surprise guest. But Hubie doesn't know what books to pick. And his team gets a late start. How can they ever expect to win?
  [1. Reading--Juvenile fiction. 2. Contests--Juvenile fiction. 3. Elementary schools--Juvenile fiction.] I. Title. II Series.
  PZ7.T3 Re 2015
  [E]--dc23
                    2015296069

978-1-61479-606-0
(reinforced library bound edition)

HUBIE →

LAUGHING OUT LOUD IS PERMITTED.

ABDO

Spotlight
A Division of ABDO
abdopublishing.com

REGULAR WORM

CONTENTS

PENNY→

READ AND LEARN.

CHAPTER 1
THE LAUNCH

Our school librarian, Mrs. Beamster, announced we were going to have a team Readathon.

She explained the rules. "The class is going to split up into two teams. Whichever team reads the most amount of books in five days will win."

RING.

OH, GREAT.

I SMELL PIZZA.

I raised my hand.

"Yes, Hubie," said Mrs. Beamster.

"What do we win?" I asked.

"The winning team will have lunch with a special author who is coming to visit next week."

RHINOCEROS

Eric raised his hand.

"Yes, Eric," said Mrs. Beamster.

"What are we having for lunch?" asked Eric.

ERIC
BEING
OBNOXIOUS

"That's not the point," said Mrs. Beamster. "It's about spending time with a real live author."

"I'd rather spend time with a real live pizza," giggled Eric.

PEPPERONI
AND
BEEF

9

ASTRO-ANT →

CHAPTER 2

TAKING SIDES

"We have to choose up the teams," said Mrs. Beamster.

"I want to be on a team with Hubie, Derek, Freddy, and Randy," said Eric.

"That leaves Penny and Doris," said Mrs. Beamster, "that's five against two."

ARE YOU SCARED, GIRLS?

"No problem," said Penny. "We can out-read the boys even if it was a hundred of them against us two."

"Oh, yeah?" snarled Eric.

"Absolutely." Penny smiled and gave Doris a high five.

"Okay," said Mrs. Beamster. "The Readathon is officially on!"

CHAPTER 3
THE NAME GAME

"We need a team name," I said.

"What about 'The Dudes'?" said Eric.

"What about 'The Duds'?" said Penny.

"Very funny," said Eric.

"Not as funny as you winning," said Penny.

"We'll just see!" snarled Eric.

"Well, we'll be 'The Champs,'" bragged Penny.

"More like 'The Chumps,'" snickered Derek.

"We'll be 'The Kings,'" said Eric.

"And we'll be 'The Pages,'" laughed Doris.

14

DON'T MOVE! LOOK LIKE A PERIOD.

CHAPTER 4
CHECK 'EM OUT

Penny and Doris each checked out an armful of books.

"We better check out some books, too," said Freddy.

"Tomorrow," said Eric, "we have baseball practice today."

But when tomorrow came, Derek invited The Kings over to play video games.

17

By the third day, the score was:
The Pages: five books.
The Kings: zero books.
"We better start reading," I
said.

"No sweat," said Eric. "When we want to, we can pass them, and besides, my favorite TV show is on tonight."

By the fourth day, the score was:

The Pages: nine books.

The Kings: zero books.

CHAPTER 5
DESPERATE MEASURES

"This is getting serious," I said.

"No sweat," said Eric. "I'll check out twenty picture books."

"I don't think they count those," I said. "They want books with lots of words."

ERIC, QUIT SAYING "NO SWEAT."

WELL, EXCUSE ME.

YEAH, IT'S GETTING OLD.

"What about comic books?" asked Derek.

"Chapter books and novels," I said. "I think we should declare a turn-off-the-TV week."

"Hey, that is serious. I'll go into heavy withdrawal symptoms!" whined Eric.

"Well, if we don't, our chances of winning will go down the tube," I said. Then I checked out an armful of books.

THESE BOOKS ARE DUE IN TWO WEEKS. DO YOU NEED A COUPLE OF FIFTH GRADERS TO CARRY THEM FOR YOU?
NO THANKS.

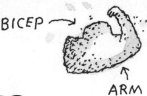
BICEP →
ARM

CHAPTER 6
HEAVY READING

"You're building up your arms," snickered Penny. "Too bad you're not building up your mind."

"My mind is fine," I answered.

"That's right," said Penny. "You're a muscle head."

By the time I got home, I was too tired from carrying all those books, so I took a nap.

SLEEPY HEAD ⟶

25

CHAPTER 7

A DEEP THINKER

After dinner I took the top book off the pile and started reading. It was *20,000 Leagues Under the Sea* by Jules Verne. By bedtime, I had plowed through nine pages.

27

A LEAGUE IS 3 MILES.

"You're doing fine, Hubie," said Mom.

"Yeah, but I still have 19,000 Leagues to go."

"Stick with it, Hubie. Just keep diving in."

I hope I don't drown.

TURN THE LIGHTS OUT, HUBIE, WE'VE GOT SCHOOL TOMORROW.

↑ BEDTIME SNACK

HEAVY
EYELIDS

SUBMARINE
SANDWICH

29

CHAPTER 8
20,000 LEAKS UNDER THE SEA

That night I had a dream. I was swimming in the ocean for miles and miles. I was about to drown when I came to the shore.

It was a desert. I wished it was a dessert. I was riding my dog, Tailspin, and being chased by Penny and Doris. They were throwing bookmarks at me.

BOOKMARKS

SAND ↗

31

Suddenly, I came to some mountains. But the mountains were made of books. Big books— HUGE books. There was no place to cross, no place to hide. Penny

HA, HA, HA.

HA, HA, HA.

I'M DOOMED!

and Doris caught up with me and started laughing. It was horrible. Luckily my alarm clock went off and woke me up. It was time to go to school.

BOOKMOBILE →

CHAPTER 9
READ ON

The next day the score was:
The Pages: 16 books.
The Kings: 2 ⅓ books.
The boys were desperate. They went to Mrs. Beamster.

"We're desperate!" I said. "We need to find books we will like."

THE KINGS ARE GETTING TROUNCED.

GUYS, I'M STARTING TO SWEAT THIS.

"Have you ever read a book from the Black Lagoon?"
"Where's that?" asked Eric.

"Follow me," said Mrs. Beamster . . . so they did.

They followed her past Dr. Seuss, past *The Wild Things*.

"Here we are," smiled Mrs. Beamster. "In the Black Lagoon!" It was a shelf of chapter books.

"There's plenty for all of us. If we read all of them, we'll beat the girls easy," said Eric.

I DIDN'T EVEN KNOW THIS PART OF THE LIBRARY EXISTED.

WHERE IS SHE TAKING US?

We started pulling out books from the shelves.

"I've got *The Class Trip from the Black Lagoon*," said Derek.

"I've got *The Science Fair*," said Randy.

"I've got *The Little League Team*," said Derek.

"I've got *The Big Game*," said Eric.

"I've got all the rest," I said, filling my arms with books.

"Happy reading," smiled Mrs. Beamster as she checked them out.

DOC, CAN YOU CHECK ME OUT?

NO, YOU'LL NEED A LIBRARIAN FOR THAT.

COOTIES

CHAPTER 10
HOOKED AND BOOKED

I read right through lunch and recess. I read on the bus. I read on the couch. I read during and after dinner. I read in bed. I couldn't stop reading.

There was something strangely
familiar about these books.

The next day in class everyone had read their books. The score was:

The Pages: 26 books.
The Kings: 26 books.

I DEMAND A RECOUNT!

I'VE NEVER BEEN SO HUMILIATED.

"It looks like a tie," said Mrs. Beamster. "I guess you'll all get to have lunch with the author."

CHAPTER 11
THE BIG DAY

That Friday, the author came. He was the Author from the Black Lagoon. He looked normal, except for a few odd things. He had yellow shoes, a yellow shirt, a yellow hat, and a black and yellow car.

"What's your favorite color?" asked Eric.

"Blue," the author smiled. "Just kidding. My favorite color is yellow."

HE LOOKS FAMILIAR.

FISH BOY →

"Why?" asked Penny.

"What's your favorite color?" asked the author.

"Pink," said Penny.

"Why?" asked the author.

"It just makes me feel good," said Penny.

"There you have it," said the author. "What's your name?"

"I'm Penny," said Penny.

"I'm Doris," said Doris.

"I'm Eric," said Eric.

"I'm Derek," said Derek.

"I'm Freddy," said Freddy.

← PENNY

"Then you must be Hubie," smiled the author.

"How did you know?" I asked.

"I have a strange feeling we've met before," smiled the author.

49

"Me too," I said.

"What's for lunch?" asked Eric.

"What would you like?" asked the author.

"Pizza," said all the kids.

"Pizza it is," said the author.

"With pepperoni, meatballs, and sausage?" asked Eric.

"Sure," said the author, "when you write a story—anything is possible."

51

CHAPTER 12
LUNCH

Lunch was great! The pizza was perfect and the author told us how he always wanted to be a writer. And how we are all special and should follow our own dreams.

I asked him if he was working on any new books.

He said he was working on a new chapter book called *The Reading Challenge from the Black Lagoon.*

"Will you write about us?" asked Penny.

"It's quite possible," winked the author.

We were all sad when he had to go.

As he drove off in his black and yellow car, I had the same feeling that we had met before. Like the author said, "With imagination, all things are possible."

THANKS FOR COMING.

YOU DIDN'T TELL US YOUR NAME.

55

THE HISTORY OF BOOKS

People have been writing on "things" for a long time. However, in human history, books are fairly recent. That is mainly because early man didn't have paper. Cavemen started writing on walls, which is still done in some places.

PLEASE DON'T MOVE.

In 3100 B.C., Mesopotamians started writing on clay tablets. 3,000 years later, early Romans wrote on wax tablets. On a hot day, your book might melt before you got it home from the library.

Ancient Egyptians wrote on papyrus, which was made from the stems of plants, so you could grow your own book!

Longer pieces of papyrus were rolled up by the early Greeks and called "scrolls." These scrolls were the beginning of books.

The first library was started in Alexandria, in the 3rd century B.C. If you have an overdue book from this library—you have a huge fine!

Around the 3rd century B.C. papyrus was replaced by parchment, which was made from the skins of animals.

The Mayans also wrote on scrolls.

Paper was invented in China around the first century. Also, the first printing of books started in China during the Tang dynasty (618–907).

In Europe, most books were copied by hand, until around the year 1440 when Johannes Gutenberg invented the printing press. That made books available to a larger number of people.

Today, we have the electronic book, or "e-book."

But whatever way people use to record their information and imaginations, the most important thing will always be your ability and desire to read it.

BOOK RIDDLES

1. What's the tallest building in every town?
   The library. It has lots of stories.

2. What color is a book when you finish it?
   Red.

MOM, I FINISHED MY BOOK AND IT WAS TERRIFIC.

3. Why are books never cold?
   Because they're always under the covers.

4. Why are libraries magical?
   Because there's an elf in every shelf.

5. Why do books make you feel like a king?

Because they are full of pages.

6. How is a clarinet similar to a book?

They both need a read.